LIFE SCIENCE

ANIMALS

Lauri Seidlitz

WEIGL PUBLISHERS INC.

Project Coordinator
Heather C. Hudak

Design
Bryan Pezzi

Cover Design
Terry Paulhus

Published by Weigl Publishers Inc.
350 5th Avenue, Suite 3304, PMB 6G
New York, NY 10118-0069

Website: www.weigl.com
Copyright ©2008 WEIGL PUBLISHERS INC.

All of the Internet URLs given in the book were valid at the time of publication. However, due to the dynamic nature of the Internet, some addresses may have changed, or sites may have ceased to exist since publication. While the author and publisher regret any inconvenience this may cause readers, no responsibility for any such changes can be accepted by either the author or the publisher.

Library of Congress Cataloging-in-Publication Data

Seidlitz, Lauri.
  Animals / Lauri Seidlitz.
      p. cm. -- (Life science)
  Includes index.
  ISBN 978-1-59036-701-8 (hard cover : alk. paper) -- ISBN 978-1-59036-702-5 (soft cover : alk. paper)
  1. Animals--Juvenile literature. I. Title.
  QL49.S337 2008
  590--dc22
                                        2007012615

Printed in the United States of America
1 2 3 4 5 6 7 8 9 0 11 10 09 08 07

Every reasonable effort has been made to trace ownership and to obtain permission to reprint copyright material. The publishers would be pleased to have any errors or omissions brought to their attention so that they may be corrected in subsequent printings.

Contents

What Do You Know about Animals?

Most living things on Earth are plants or animals. Both plants and animals need **oxygen**, and both grow and change during their life cycles. The main difference between plants and animals is that animals have to find food to eat. Plants make their own food using sunlight, water, **carbon dioxide**, and nutrients in the soil. Animals must get food from the plants and other animals around them.

Millions of different kinds of animals live on Earth.
Scientists divide all animals into two main groups.

Vertebrates
Vertebrates are animals that
have a backbone.

Invertebrates
Invertebrates are animals that
do not have a backbone.

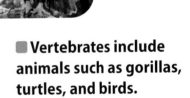

■ **Vertebrates include
animals such as gorillas,
turtles, and birds.**

■ **Invertebrates
include animals
such as octopuses,
spiders, and crabs.**

Puzzler
How many animals can you
name in a minute? Time
yourself with a partner.

5

Life Cycles

All living things have a life cycle that includes birth, growth, **reproduction**, and death. An animal will go through many changes during its life cycle.

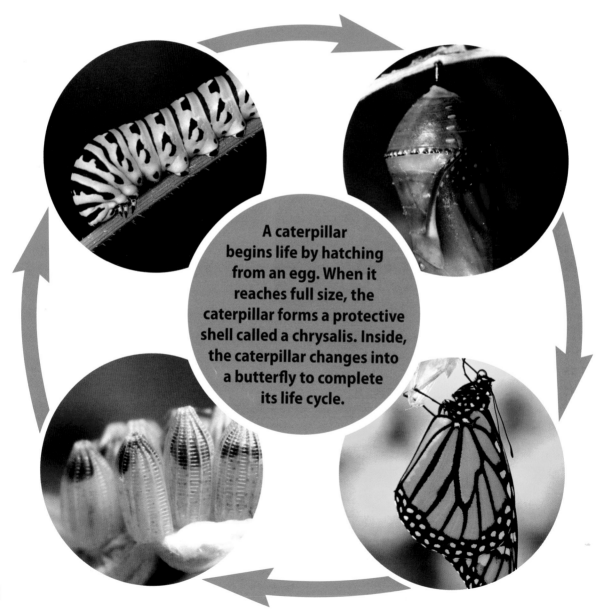

A caterpillar begins life by hatching from an egg. When it reaches full size, the caterpillar forms a protective shell called a chrysalis. Inside, the caterpillar changes into a butterfly to complete its life cycle.

Young bald eagles grow very quickly, but they do not get their adult colors until they are four or five years old.

Some animals are born live. Others hatch from eggs. Great white sharks are hatched from eggs inside the mother's body.

The brown bear stays with its mother for several years until it learns to find food and take care of itself.

Activity

Make a Collage

Make a **collage** of the life of someone in your family. You could start with a baby picture. How has this person changed over time?

Animal Types

Mammals, reptiles, fish, birds, amphibians, and insects are different types of animals. Do you know what makes each one special?

Types

Mammals	Reptiles	Fish
• drink milk from their mothers • have fur or hair • most young are born live	• most hatch from eggs • have scaly skin • need the Sun to keep their bodies warm	• breathe using gills • live in the water • use tails and fins to swim

Examples cows, dogs, elephants

Examples crocodiles, lizards, snakes

Examples cod, salmon, tuna

Puzzler

What type of animal is a whale?

Clues: It lives its entire life in the ocean and is mostly hairless. It breathes through a blowhole on the top of its head. It gives birth to live young. A young whale drinks milk from its mother.

Answer: Whales are mammals. Dolphins and seals are other mammals that live in the water.

Birds	Amphibians	Insects
• have feathers and wings • lay eggs • most can fly	• live on land and in water • need the Sun to keep their bodies warm	• have hard shells on the outside of their bodies • have six legs • some have wings and can fly

Examples geese, parrots, robins

Examples frogs, salamanders, toads

Examples flies, ladybugs, mosquitoes

Has Your Pet Met a Vet?

A veterinarian is a doctor who takes care of sick animals. Veterinarians are also known as vets. If you want to become a vet, you have to go to a university and study veterinary medicine. Vets treat many different animals. Some vets specialize in one group of animals, such as small animals or farm animals. Would you like to be a veterinarian?

■ Dogs are just one kind of animal that vets treat.

■ Veterinarians keep farm animals, such as horses and pigs, healthy.

Activity

Do Your Own Research

Have a teacher or parent help you find out more about these animal careers:

• animal health technologist
• animal trainer
• dog groomer
• kennel owner
• wildlife biologist
• wildlife rehabilitator
• wildlife photographer
• zookeeper

Classifying Animals

You can **classify** animals into types. By comparing animals with one another, you can learn to group similar creatures.

Look for

Movement	Body Parts	Shape & Size	Body Covering
flies, hops, runs, slithers, walks	ears, eyes, fins, head, hoofs, legs, neck, paws, tail, teeth, tongue, wings	flat, large, streamlined, tall, tiny	feathers, fur, hair, scales, shell, skin

Activity

Design an Animal

Create a new animal. Draw or paint the animal using features from the groups below.

Homes	Protection	Food	Color
caves, ground, houses, nests, trees, water	beak, claws, flight, horns, quills, shell, smell, stinger, taste, teeth	eggs, fish, insects, plants, other animals	black, blue, brown, gray, green, white

Everyday Animals

Many animals live with or near people. Pets live with their owners, and they depend on people to feed and take care of them. You may see or hear animals in your yard or on the way to school. Animals such as squirrels, bees, and worms often live near people, but take care of themselves.

■ Some dogs are trained to help people with special needs.

Some animals help people or do work for them. Farm animals, such as chickens and cows, provide food. Sheep provide wool for clothing. Horses and dogs often help farmers do their work. Animals that live on farms depend on their owners for food and shelter.

■ Horses are strong. They sometimes work for people by pulling heavy objects.

Activity

Use Your Five Senses to Explore Animals

Your senses are your best tools for exploring the world around you.

You can **see** a bird's nest in a tree.
You can **hear** a wasp buzzing in the garden.
You can **feel** a fly land on your hand.
You might **smell** a skunk when you are camping.
When you **taste** honey, you think of a bee.

1. Spend one hour outside observing the world around you with all your senses.
2. Write down the name of every animal you sense.
3. Write down how you knew they were there.
4. Draw a picture of yourself and the animals you sensed.
5. Label each of your senses on your drawing.

Animals in Nature

In nature, animals survive best without any contact with humans. They find everything they need in their surroundings. Some animals learn how to survive from their mothers and members of their social group. Elephants, wolves, and lions learn this way.

■ **Lions relax up to 21 hours a day.**

Instinct

Animals know how to survive by **instinct**. This means they are born with knowledge to help them survive. Fish hatch from eggs and immediately live on their own. They do not need their parents to teach them how to survive.

■ Proboscis monkeys have a large nose. They honk their nose when they sense danger.

■ Salmon have a strong instinct to leave the ocean to lay their eggs. They return to the freshwater streams where they hatched.

Puzzler

Why should you avoid feeding animals in nature?

Answer: In nature, animals get everything they need from their environment. They can rely on humans too much for food and survival. Feeding food, such as popcorn or bread, to wild animals means they are not eating foods that are healthy for them.

Habitat

A nimals live in almost every corner of the world. Even the hottest and coldest places on Earth make good homes for some animals. Different animals have **adapted** to different locations. They have special features that make them well suited to their natural **habitat**.

Temperate Forest

Temperate forest animals have adapted to live in areas where there are cold winters and hot summers. Black bears have a heavy fur coat that helps keep them warm in the winter.

Tropical Forest

Tropical forest animals have adapted to a habitat with tall trees high above the ground. Gibbons have long arms and legs that help them travel high above the forest floor through the tops of trees. They rarely go down to the ground.

Mountain

Mountain animals are adapted to cool temperatures and steep slopes. Mountain goats have hoofs that grip rocky slopes.

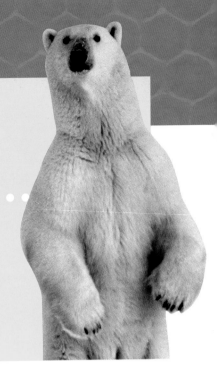

Puzzler

Could a polar bear live in a tropical rain forest?

Answer: If a polar bear tried to live in a rain forest, it would have trouble getting enough food. Its white fur would stand out against the green plants, and its prey would easily see it and escape. Hot temperatures and heavy rain would make its thick fur wet, hot, and uncomfortable.

Polar

Polar animals have adapted to cold temperatures, ice, and snow. Polar bears have black skin under their white fur. This attracts sunlight and helps keep them warm.

Grassland

Grassland animals have adapted to large, open spaces. Cheetahs are able to run fast across open grasslands to catch their prey. They are the fastest land animals in the world.

Desert

Desert animals have adapted to heat and scarce water. Camels can survive 10 days without water.

Ocean

Ocean animals have adapted to life in the water. Fish breathe through gills that remove oxygen from water.

The Muskox Needs No Sox

The muskox is perfectly clothed to live in its cold habitat. The muskox's coat has two layers. The inner coat is a thick fleece, as soft as the finest wool. This layer, like the down on ducks, provides **insulation**. The outer layer is made of long, coarse guard hairs that provide an outer "curtain" to block the wind. These hairs can be long enough to reach the ground.

■ Muskox have a woolly undergrowth that is up to 10 times warmer than sheep wool.

Other animals have adapted to cold habitats. Many animals, including deer and mountain goats, grow a thick layer of fur each winter and lose it in the spring when it is no longer needed. This loss of hair is called molting.

Puzzler

The wolf also has layers of fur like the muskox. What can you guess about the habitat of wolves?

Answer: Wolves also live in areas with cold temperatures.

Protection and Camouflage

M any animals have some form of natural camouflage. One type of **camouflage** might be an animal's fur or skin, which blends in with the colors and patterns of the animal's surroundings. Camouflage makes the animal difficult to see. This ability to hide helps both the animals that hunt for food and those that are hunted.

■ **The arctic fox's fur changes from white in the winter to brown in the summer. This keeps the fox camouflaged all year long.**

Camouflage is not the only way to avoid being hunted. Many animals have ways to protect themselves against danger. Some are equipped to fight. Animals that fight sometimes have sharp teeth, long claws, horns, quills, or great strength. Other animals avoid danger by flying or running away. Animals that flee danger often have excellent eyesight, sense of smell, or hearing to give them advance warning of danger.

I am a mammal. My teeth are sharp, and my whiskers are long. I have four legs and a tail. My stripes help me blend in with grass and trees. What am I?

Answer: A tiger

■ **Most birds depend on sharp eyesight and their ability to fly to avoid danger.**

23

Web of Life

All of the plants and animals in a habitat depend on one another for survival. Everything contributes something to and takes something from its environment. Each animal gives and takes in just the right amounts so the habitat stays in balance.

■ Chipmunks eat seeds, grains, berries, and nuts. They hold food in their front feet and chew it with their sharp front teeth.

Food chains form when one animal eats another animal or a plant. Energy moves from the thing that is eaten to the thing that eats it. A food web forms when many food chains are connected.

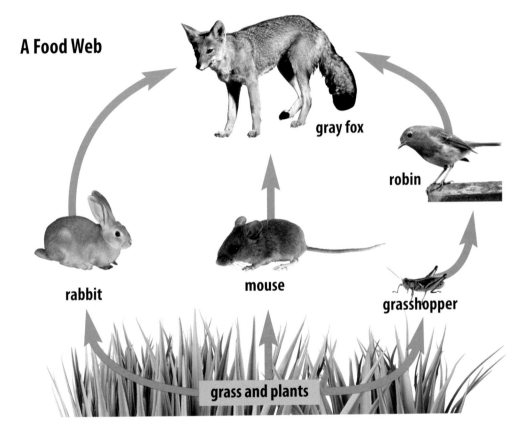

A Food Web

gray fox

robin

rabbit

mouse

grasshopper

grass and plants

Puzzler

Foxes do not eat plants. Do you think anything would happen to this gray fox if all the plants in its habitat died?

Answer: Yes. The rabbit, mouse, bird, and grasshopper would move away if the plants died because they would have no food to eat. The gray fox would also have to move, or it would go hungry.

Animal Roles

Wolves use their jaws and molars to crush bones. They can bite through a moose's upper hind leg in six to eight bites.

Animals play many roles in the web of life. Herbivores eat plants that grow from energy the Sun provides. Carnivores eat other animals. Omnivores eat both plants and animals. Scavengers find and eat dead animals. **Decomposers** break down rotting plants and animals to make nutrients for plants.

Some of a panda's teeth wear down from eating bamboo stems.

Animal teeth are a good clue to what animals eat. Carnivores, such as wolves, have sharp, pointed teeth that are good for tearing flesh. Herbivores, such as elephants, have flat teeth that are good for grinding plant fibers. Omnivores, such as the black bear, have both kinds of teeth.

■ **The lion lives and hunts in a group called a pride.**

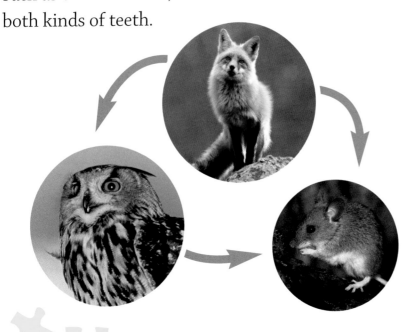

Prey are animals that other animals eat. Predators are animals that hunt other animals for food. Many animals are both predators and prey. For example, an owl hunts and eats mice, but this same owl might be hunted and eaten by a fox.

Puzzler

Do you think the dinosaur *Tyrannosaurus rex* was a predator or prey animal? What characteristics are your proof?

Answer: The Tyrannosaurus rex's many sharp teeth are a good clue that it was a powerful predator.

27

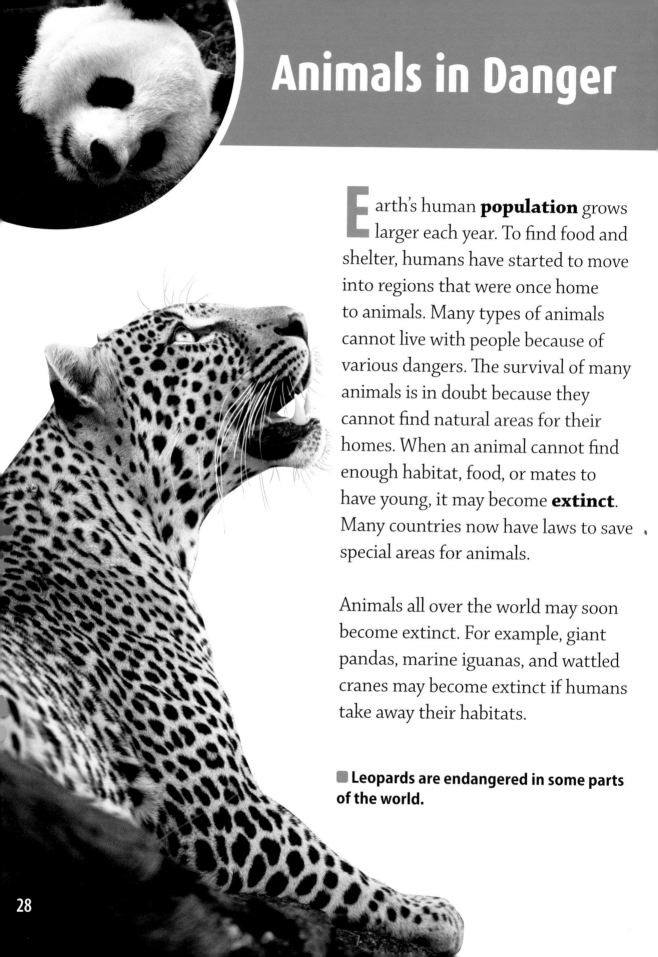

Animals in Danger

Earth's human **population** grows larger each year. To find food and shelter, humans have started to move into regions that were once home to animals. Many types of animals cannot live with people because of various dangers. The survival of many animals is in doubt because they cannot find natural areas for their homes. When an animal cannot find enough habitat, food, or mates to have young, it may become **extinct**. Many countries now have laws to save special areas for animals.

Animals all over the world may soon become extinct. For example, giant pandas, marine iguanas, and wattled cranes may become extinct if humans take away their habitats.

■ **Leopards are endangered in some parts of the world.**

■ Overhunting is causing the numbers of green sea turtles and tigers to decline.

If you go into a place where animals live, you can help them survive by following a few rules:

1. Do not leave food or other garbage around. Animals are healthiest if they eat food that lives or grows naturally in their habitat.

2. Do not touch or go near young birds or other animals that you find in nature. Their mother could be nearby and frightened away from her young.

3. Never try to pet an animal in nature, even if it is very young. It may be frightened and hurt you, or its mother may hurt you while trying to protect her young.

Use Your Senses

Sight, hearing, touch, smell, and taste are senses you use every day, but common sense is just as important. Common sense means using your brain. Use your common sense to match the following labels with the most appropriate animal.

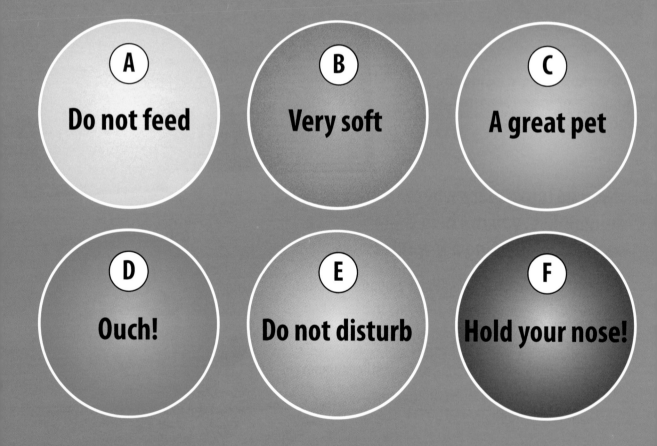

A Do not feed

B Very soft

C A great pet

D Ouch!

E Do not disturb

F Hold your nose!

31

Glossary

adapted: having become suited to a certain environment or way of life by changing gradually over a long period of time

camouflage: a disguise that helps plants, animals, and humans blend in with their natural surroundings

carbon dioxide: a colorless, odorless gas

classify: to arrange plants and animals into groups by comparing how they are alike

collage: a collection and display of different objects or materials

decomposers: living things, such as bacteria and mushrooms, that digest the remains of dead plants and animals

extinct: no longer in existence

habitat: the place where an animal or plant is known to live or grow

instinct: knowledge or ability that an animal has at birth

insulation: a layer of material that prevents heat loss

oxygen: a gas found in water and air

population: the total number of people, plants, or animals in an area

reproduction: the way animals produce young

Index

Websites

www.worldwildlife.org/endangered
www.bbc.co.uk/nature/animals

www3.nationalgeographic.com/animals
www.sandiegozoo.org

Some websites stay current longer than others. For further websites, use your search engines to locate the following topics: marine life, pets, reptiles, wild animals, and zoos.